Aaa!
Monster Hunter's
Guide to Monsters

So you want to be a Monster Hunter! Then this is the book for YOU, with everything you need to know about Monsters: what they look like, where they live, and – Most Important of All – How To Deal With Them!

Also in Red Fox by Jim and Duncan Eldridge

Bogeys, Boils and Bellybuttons
How to Handle Grown-Ups
More Ways to Handle Grown-Ups
What Grown-Ups Say and What They Really
Mean
The Complete How to Handle Grown-Ups

And by Jim Eldridge
The Completely Misleading Guide to School

AAARGH!
THE
MONSTER HUNTER'S GUIDE

RED FOX

Published by Random House Children's Books
20 Vauxhall Bridge Road, London SW1V 2SA

A division of Random House UK Ltd
London Melbourne Sydney Auckland
Johannesburg and agencies throughout the world

Text © Jim & Duncan Eldridge 1994
Illustrations © Harry Venning 1994

1 3 5 7 9 10 8 6 4 2

First published by Red Fox 1994

Set in Present Roman and New Century Schoolbook by
Intype, London
Printed and bound in Great Britain by
Cox & Wyman Ltd, Reading, Berkshire

RANDOM HOUSE UK Limited Reg. No. 954009

ISBN 0 09 928651 3

Contents

INTRODUCTION

So you want to be a Monster Hunter! Then this is the book for YOU, with everything you need to know about monsters: what they look like, where they live, and – Most Important Of All – How To Deal With Them!

There are those people who say that you shouldn't hunt monsters in the first place, that they should be left alone. Well that may be all right for those people, but it's not all right for those of you who are constantly under threat from monsters:

– Those of you who have relatives who are vampires in disguise

– Those of you with a neighbour whose dog is really a werewolf

– Those of you who live next to a pyramid and are always in fear of being attacked by a mummy

And for those of you who scoff and say, 'I'm safe, I've got nothing to worry about'. HOW CAN YOU BE SO SURE?

Do you ever look at your dad and notice that his eyes are bloodshot? Does he ever go out AT NIGHT? If the answer to these two questions is yes, then ask yourself: Is it because he is really a VAMPIRE?!

And that blob that looks just like wet soap on the side of the basin in your bathroom. Are you sure it's just soap? Could it be a BLOB that's crept up from the Underworld, up the drain, into your bathroom and is now sitting there waiting to take over your body and then take over the world?

And have you ever stood somewhere and thought to yourself – 'Pooh! There's a terrible smell in here, like something rotten!' Could it be that the smell is coming from a ZOMBIE hiding around a corner, just waiting to pounce on you and eat you?

And that time you looked in a mirror and thought you saw something behind you, but when you turned round there was nothing there. Could it be a

GHOST trying to get in touch with you?

Don't hide from THE TRUTH. Use this book as your 'Guide To Discover Who The Monsters Are' and, how to defend yourself against them!

(BUT BE WARNED! Monsters are everywhere, and they can be Dangerous!).

1
VAMPIRES

WHAT IS A VAMPIRE?

A vampire is an Undead Person. This means they appear to be dead, but they are in fact half-alive, or not, as the case may be.

Vampires can live for ever, but can only go out at night as being in daylight is harmful to their health (they turn into dust, which is not a healthy thing to happen to anyone).

They get their energy by sucking the blood out of living creatures, usually human beings. A farmer who had turned into a vampire once took to sucking blood out of his cows because there were no human beings around. He had the most unusual herd of cows ever, with great big fangs and each one afraid of daylight.

Once a vampire has sucked a person's blood, that person turns into a vampire as well. In fact, if a vampire sucks anything then it turns into a vampire and will live for ever. So watch out if you ever see a vampire sucking a mint or a sweet, because that sweet will turn into a vampire and will start to roam the streets looking for other sweets to suck.

Vampires are able to turn into bats. This usually means the sort of black flying animal that hangs upside down in caves. However, there was one vampire who wasn't very bright, and on being told that he had to turn into a bat, he turned into a cricket bat and was badly bashed up for two innings while being used by the England Cricket Team in a test match against Australia. The fact that this test match was also held in bright sunlight made matters worse, because as the third innings began, the batsman was surprised to find his bat had turned into dust. The result was that the vampire lost his undead 'life' and England lost the Ashes (both sorts; the real Ashes, and also the dusty ashes of the vampire, which blew away in the wind.)

Vampires often have strange-sounding names like Count Rekcusdoolb. This is useful for any Vampire Hunters in the area, as they will notice that if the Count's name is spelt backwards it will reveal that they are really ... AAAAARGHHH!!

In the Transylvanian telephone book there are thousands of people with the surname Alucard. However, this does not necessarily mean that they are vampires, it just means that if you've got any sense you'll avoid them — especially at night.

WHERE VAMPIRES CAN BE FOUND

Vampires have to sleep in a coffin, so this means their house or flat has to be big enough to put a coffin in. As most visitors will notice if there is a large coffin in the living room or in the kitchen, most vampires prefer to live in a place that has a cellar where they can hide their coffin. For this reason it is unlikely that a vampire will live on the twelfth floor of a block of flats. However, as anything is possible, if you know someone who lives in a block of flats and keeps a coffin in their kitchen or bedroom, then be warned. After all, it would not be a good idea to let them sharpen their teeth on your neck!

HOW TO DEAL WITH VAMPIRES

To get rid of a vampire it is best to hammer a wooden stake through the vampire's heart. (Note: this is best done when the vampire is fast asleep as they are unlikely to stand still and let you do it.)

Vampires can also be turned into a pile of dust by:

- A cross or crucifix

- Garlic

- Water

- Mirrors

- Having their heads cut off

- School dinners

THE VAMPIRE WHO COULDN'T STAND THE SIGHT OF BLOOD

Count Vun To Ten was a vegetarian vampire who hated meat of any kind, and especially hated the thought of drinking blood. This caused him lots of trouble at family reunions when his Great Grandmother, Countess Eva Brick, would tell him off for letting the family down by not having any blood trickling from his fangs. Count Vun To Ten solved the problem by sucking the juice very savagely out of a kilo of tomatoes whenever he was due to meet his Great Grandmother.

THE VAMPIRE WHO WAS AFRAID OF THE DARK

Little Count Drak was a nephew of the famous Count Dracula and his family had high hopes of him becoming one of the most famous vampires of all time. Unfortunately Little Count Drak was afraid of the dark and was scared to go out at night. This made it difficult for him to be a successful vampire as, if he were to go out during the day hunting his victims, he would almost certainly turn into a pile of dust. His family tried to solve the problem by giving him a large torch. This worked for a while. Little Count Drak would hang around dark streets with his torch and wait for an unsuspecting passer-by to walk past so he could jump on them and bite them on the neck. Unfortunately for him, his shining torch gave the game away as people could see him coming from miles away.

Then one day a terrible tragedy happened: his batteries ran down and his torch went out. Little Count Drak was so frightened that he fainted, and by the time he woke up it was daylight, and he just had time to say, 'Uh oh! That looks like sunshine . . .!' before he turned into a pile of dust.

THE VAMPIRE WITH FALSE TEETH

Count Bakwurdz was only ten when he had an accident on his bicycle that knocked out all his teeth. This meant that he was doomed to spend his life unable to bite holes in people's necks. At first he tried just sucking his victims' necks, but without the vital puncture hole, all that happened was his intended victim got a big red mark on their neck, and Count Bakwurdz strained all his jaw muscles and had to go around with a big bandage around the bottom half of his head.

In desperation he phoned different dentists and asked them to make him a set of false teeth, but all the dentists were suspicious because the Count could only come for an appointment when it was dark. In the end the Count bought himself a set of Vampire Fangs

from a late-night toy shop. 'At last,' he said, 'now I can bite someone!' Off he went that night, grabbed the first person he met, and took a bite.

Unfortunately for the Count, the plastic that the toy teeth were made of was very thin and, as the fangs hit his intended victim's neck, they bent and punctured his own lower lip instead. Count Bakwurdz didn't realize what had happened. He was so pleased that at last he had a taste of real blood, that he sucked as hard as he could and sucked out all his own blood.

By the time he realized what he had done, and that there was a long delay before the blood in his stomach could get back into his system, it was too late. He fainted from loss of blood and by the time he woke up it was dawn and ... AAAAARGHHH!! It was 'pile of dust' time again!

THE VAMPIRE WHO ENDED UP IN ORBIT AROUND THE EARTH

Count Zammo was creeping round a fair one night looking for victims, when he saw a poster saying, FAT FRED – THE FATTEST MAN IN THE WHOLE WORLD, with a picture of a man who looked like an elephant in a shirt and trousers.

'Fantastic!' said Zammo. 'What a body! That man will have enough blood in him to keep me filled up for months!'

So Zammo crept off to the tent where Fat Fred was on show. Luckily for Zammo, no one else was interested in going to see Fat Fred, so Zammo found himself all alone with this huge enormous man. Zammo stared at Fat Fred with wonder in his eyes.

'What are you looking at?' demanded Fat Fred.

'You!' said Zammo, and he leapt upon Fat Fred and bit him on the neck.

Unluckily for Zammo, what he didn't know was that Fat Fred was actually a fake fat person who wore an inflatable suit beneath his clothes. When Zammo's teeth bit into what he thought was Fred's neck, he punctured the inflatable suit. Next second... Woooooooooosh!!

Luckily for Fat Fred (now Very Thin Fred), he fell out of the suit, while poor Zammo hurtled up into the sky, his teeth firmly stuck in the fast-deflating inflatable suit.

By the time the suit had finished deflating, Zammo had reached the upper limits of the Earth's atmosphere. Being a vampire and unable to be killed (except by the methods previously mentioned), Zammo then went into orbit around the Earth. To this day, Count Zammo still goes round and round the Earth, doing his best to avoid being hit by satellites and rockets.

As for Fat Fred, he simply bought himself another inflatable suit, but now there is a new sign by his tent that says: FAT FRED – THE FATTEST MAN IN THE WHOLE WORLD – ONLY PEOPLE WITHOUT TEETH ADMITTED.

Did you know that the reason Vampires always look so untidy and have such terrible hairstyles is because they don't cast a reflection, so they can never look in a mirror and see what they look like.

Did you know that if you say 'Vampire' backwards it sounds totally meaningless, so don't bother.

'Mummy, Mummy, the other kids at school make fun of me! They say I look like a vampire.'

'Ignore them, son, and eat your soup before it clots.'

2

WEREWOLVES

WHAT IS A WEREWOLF?

Werewolves are people who look quite ordinary but turn into wolves every time there's a full moon.

Most people who have been identified as werewolves by their neighbours are often embarrassed and try to pretend that they have been cured and are no longer werewolves. The fact that they are lying is shown if you challenge them on the night of the full moon, and they say, 'OK, I admit it, I used to be a werewolf but I'm cured and I'm all right naaaoooooowwwwwwwwwww!!! Woof woof!'

The traditional way of getting rid of a werewolf was to shoot it with a silver bullet. This used to be standard practice until the RSPCA received so many complaints from the families and owners of werewolves (plus many from werewolves themselves) that silver bullets were banned.

Now when a werewolf is caught it is

sent to a Werewolf Psychiatrist to talk about its problems. Coincidentally this had led to a huge rise in the numbers of psychiatrists who have disappeared.

WHERE WEREWOLVES CAN BE FOUND

During the day and most nights (those that don't have a full moon) werewolves just live ordinary lives in ordinary houses or flats, doing the things that werewolves do when they aren't being werewolves – things like sharpening their teeth.

During a full moon werewolves are best kept outside in a kennel, preferably chained up. Make sure they have plenty of water and a bone to gnaw. This will keep them happy.

On no account let a werewolf into your house on the night of a full moon be-

cause, not only will it eat everyone, but (unless it is house-trained, which is very unlikely) it will pee on the furniture.

HOW TO DEAL WITH A WEREWOLF

The best method to adopt if you meet a werewolf is to say, 'Sit!'

If it sits it means it is a well-trained werewolf. You can then lead it to the middle of the road, say, 'Sit!' again, and then say, 'Stay!' Then walk off and leave it there and wait for a large vehicle to come along and run it over.

If it does not sit when you say 'Sit!', then this means it is an untrained werewolf and you are in terrible trouble and you will most likely get eaten by it. The best thing is to stay indoors whenever there is a full moon. Unless, of course, a member of your family is a werewolf, in which case you are in BIG trouble.

If you must go out for a walk at a full moon, make sure you have a large friend with you who looks more appetizing than you do.

If you do meet a werewolf, under no circumstances try and be clever by throwing a stick for it to chase in the hope that it will go away. It will only bring the stick back to you and you will have to keep playing this game until you get so tired you can't play it any more. The werewolf will then eat you.

TOM THUMB WAS REALLY A WEREWOLF

Tom Thumb was a Very Famous Short Person. It is generally thought that he was always a short person, right from childhood. In fact when he was a teenager he was actually two metres tall. The reason he was so short as an adult was that he was actually a werewolf, and he was also very shortsighted.

One night, after a hard day's work in the kitchen of the restaurant where he worked, young and tall Tom fell fast asleep on the floor. Unfortunately for Tom it was the night of a full moon. At half past two in the morning Tom woke up feeling very hungry. Lying next to him on the floor he saw what looked like the leg of a rabbit. Assuming it to be a left-over from the restaurant, he chewed it and swallowed it. Then he burped, yawned, and stood up to leave, and promptly fell over.

It was then Tom realized that he had turned into a werewolf while asleep, and had eaten one of his own back legs! Because he had been half-asleep he hadn't noticed any pain.

There was only one thing for Tom to do. He waited until the full moon had gone and he had turned back into a human again. Then he hopped to the nearest surgeon and had his one remaining leg turned into two short legs, and so he became Tom Thumb, Very Famous Short Person (and secret werewolf).

THE WEREBUDGIE

One of the most unusual cases of a werewolf was actually a were*budgie*. This was a budgerigar named Cecil that used to go all hairy and develop fangs on the night of a full moon. Its owner got suspicious after it noticed that the other budgies that it had put in the cage to keep Cecil company had all mysteriously disappeared the morning after a full-moon night.

Cecil's owner decided not to waste any more money on buying companions for Cecil, so when the next full moon came poor Cecil found himself all hairy and with fangs and all alone in his cage. Feeling fed up he climbed out of his cage and went off to look for someone to eat.

The first creature he met was Tibbles, his owner's cat.

'Grrrarrr!' roared Cecil and bared his fangs ready to pounce.

'A mouse,' thought Tibbles, and scooped Cecil up and ate him in one mouthful.

THE WEREWOLF WHO THOUGHT HE WAS SUPERMAN

For some years Mr Clark Konk of Birmingham was convinced there was something strange about himself, because every full moon he began to feel a little odd, as if he was about to change into something. (Not 'change' as in put on a clean shirt and pants, but change altogether.)

After seeing the film *Superman* he realized what his problem was; he was really Superman and this strange feeling that came over him now and then meant that all he had to do was rush into the nearest phone box, and he would change, from being mild-mannered Clark Konk, into Superman! So, the next full moon, when the strange feeling came over him, he rushed into the nearest phone booth, spun around at supersonic speed, and then rushed out again, opened his mouth and cried, 'Aowoooooooooooow!!!!' Too late he realized that he had turned into a werewolf. He was promptly rounded up by the dog-catcher and spent the next fourteen days in the local pound.

THE WEREWOLF THAT WAS SOLD AS A GREYHOUND

In 1992 there was a freak period during which the full moon lasted for five whole nights, from a Monday to the following Friday.

On the Tuesday of that week a man called Al Ping bought a greyhound from a pet shop. Although it seemed to be very hairy for a greyhound, the pet-shop owner told Al that it was bound to win every race it ran in. That night Al entered his new greyhound in a race, and sure enough, it won.

It also won the next night (Wednesday), and Thursday, and Friday.

Al was delighted and persuaded all his friends to come and watch his greyhound run on Saturday night. His friends were so impressed by the greyhound's run of four wins that they took all their money out of the bank and bet on Al's greyhound.

That Saturday night the greyhounds were put into their traps. The electric hare was set going, the traps were opened . . . and five greyhounds rushed off after the electric hare.

Al and his friends stared at the other trap where Al's greyhound was, wondering what had gone wrong. Then out of that trap crawled a man, absolutely naked and looking very embarrassed.

The angry Al rushed over to the man and asked what he'd done with his greyhound.

'I'm very sorry,' said the man, 'but I *am* your greyhound. I work in the pet shop where you bought me, and on

Monday night when the full moon was just starting I turned into a werewolf, and because the full moon stayed so long this time I ended up stuck as one.'

'Mummy, mummy, the kids at school say I look like a werewolf.'

'Shut up, son, and comb your face.'

3

THE MUMMY

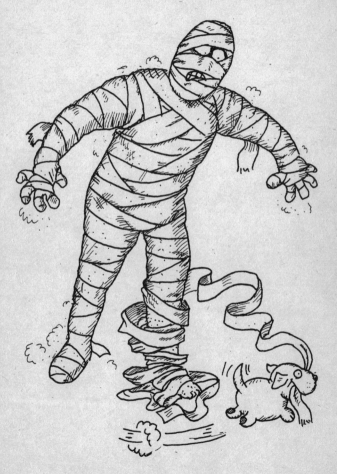

WHAT IS A MUMMY?

Most people think that a mummy is the female half of the pair of adults known as Mummy and Daddy. In most cases this is true, but what we are talking about here is a truly horrific, very tall, very muscular creature that roams around bashing people. If this *still* sounds like *your* Mummy then you are in Deep Trouble.

The mummy comes from Ancient Egypt and is usually dressed in dirty bandages. The reason the bandages are dirty is because the mummy is at least two thousand years old, and you try wearing something for two thousand years and keeping it clean!

The legend of the mummy is this; that he was a High Priest in Ancient Egypt with one of those Ancient Egyptian unpronounceable names, like Phot or Phart or Inphormation. Phot (or Phart or Inphormation) worked for a beautiful Egyptian queen and fell in love with her. Unfortunately this queen was cruel and evil and clever as well as beautiful, which was very bad luck for him (as if he didn't already have enough bad luck being called Phart) and she thought she could live for ever if, when she died, she had her priest tied up tightly with bandages, his tongue cut out, and then his body bricked up inside her pyramid with hers (dead body that is). No one is quite sure on which scientific theory the Egyptian queen based her idea, but it was either *The Egyptian Book of the Dead* or *The Raving Loony's Book of Stupid Ideas*.

So, after she died she was put inside her pyramid with her High Priest, who was all tied up with bandages and now minus his tongue, and Surprise Surprise and Lo and Behold – the Ancient Egyptian queen stayed absolutely dead!

Meanwhile, High Priest Phart stayed alive, and because pyramids have amazing powers of preservation he continued to stay alive for the next two thousand years, with nothing to do but sulk and draw Ancient Egyptian graffiti on the inside walls of the pyramid. It looked like this:

and meant: 'High Priest Phart is seriously fed up.'

Finally, in the Twentieth Century, a team of archeologists opened the pyramid up and discovered the bandaged figure of Phart. Phart opened his mouth to say 'And about time too!' but because he didn't have a tongue any more it came out as 'Aaaaarghhhh'.

This frightened the archeologists, who all ran off screaming. Phart rushed after them to tell them not to be frightened, and also to ask if they could help him take off his bandages.

He never caught up with the archeologists and ever since he has been roaming the world looking for someone to help him take his bandages off. And, because he no longer has the preserving power of the pyramid, he is gradually falling apart with bits of him falling off, which is why he nips into the nearest pyramid whenever he can to try to put off the moment when he finally turns into a pile of dust.

WHERE THE MUMMY CAN BE FOUND

Most of the time the mummy lives inside a pyramid, except when it is out and about causing mayhem and havoc. The reason why the Ancient Egyptians chose to bury their mummies inside pyramids is yet another of the Great Mysteries of All Time. There are various theories put forward for this, including:

– The very first pyramid was actually flat, but the pharaohs noticed that when it rained the roof got waterlogged and fell in. After that all pyramids were built with sloping sides so that the rain would run off.

– The pyramid design was actually a likeness in honour of Pharaoh Idjitt I, who had a pointed head.

– Originally it was intended to be a coffee-table for the gods, with the flat bit at the top and the pointed end as the leg, but the builders had the plans upside down.

HOW TO DEAL WITH A MUMMY

There is really only one way to deal with a mummy and that is to unwrap its bandages so that there is nothing holding it together, and then it will fall apart.

The trouble with this method is that you have to get close enough to the mummy to grab its bandages in the first place. This is not really a sensible idea because mummies have Superhuman Strength and will bash you if you get too close.

There is another method (not used very often), which is to call down an ancient curse on the mummy which will stop it in its tracks and cause it to fall apart. The trouble is the ancient curse takes about four and a half hours to say, and by the time you're halfway through, the mummy will have bashed you up fairly thoroughly. This is why this method is not used very often.

The best way to deal with mummies is: Avoid Them.

THE MUMMY WHO WORE STICKING-PLASTERS INSTEAD OF BANDAGES

The mummified body of a pharaoh had escaped from the British Museum and was walking around London, trying to find out the time of the next boat back to Egypt, when it noticed that its bandages were starting to come undone.

The mummy got in a bit of a panic because it knew that if its bandages fell off then it would turn into dust. It rushed into the nearest chemist shop and said, 'Quick! I need enough bandages to cover me from the top of my head to the bottom of my feet!'

The chemist was out of bandages, but said, 'Don't worry, these are even better!' and gave the mummy two hundred tins of plasters.

The mummy stuck all the plasters on, completely covering itself. Unfortunately for the mummy it had also stuck them over its eyes. Unlike its bandages, it couldn't see through the plasters. It stepped out of the chemist's shop into the road, and was run over by a bus.

THE 'NOT-QUITE' MUMMY

Workers were repairing one of the pyramids after an excavation, when suddenly they saw a figure stumbling towards them, arms outstretched, completely encased in white, and moaning.

'It's a mummy!' they screamed, and all started taking photographs of it, and then ran away, before the mummy could get them. Next day, all the news-

papers around the world had the story, and by then it was too late to tell everyone the truth, which was this: one of the workmen who was replastering the ceiling of the tomb in the middle of the pyramid had fallen into a bucket of plaster, and was trying to get his friends to take off the wet plaster before it set!

Did you know that Mummies almost died out because they didn't have any Daddies.

The mummy went into a burger bar one day and asked for a burger. The manager was shocked to see the mummy, but he served it anyway. When the mummy asked how much, the manager thought, this mummy's thousands of years old! It won't know anything about money, and said, 'That'll be twenty pounds.'

The mummy reached into its bandages, pulled out a twenty-pound note and paid up.

The manager then stared at the mummy as it ate the burger. 'I hope you don't mind me staring,' he said, 'but you're the first mummy who's ever come in here.'

'I'm not surprised, at these prices!' said the mummy.

'Mummy, Mummy, can I go out?'

'No, it's cold in this pyramid – you'll have to stay alight a little bit longer.'

4
FRANKENSTEIN'S MONSTER

WHAT IS FRANKENSTEIN'S MONSTER?

Once upon a time there lived a man called Dr Frankenstein. As a child he had been given Lego to play with and had made loads of different things (a house, a giraffe, etc). He had such fun making things that when he grew up he decided he wanted to make a human being. And not just one out of Lego, but a human being that actually moved!

Because he had trouble buying the bits he wanted in the shops, he went around graveyards at night and dug up dead bodies, cut off the bits that weren't too badly damaged, and sewed them together. Then he connected the completed body to a lot of wires, fixed the wires to a lightning conductor, and waited for a storm to come and bring life to his creation.

He waited and he waited and he

waited, but unluckily for Dr Frankenstein, the weather was brilliant for weeks and weeks and weeks, and no storm happened. Every night he turned on his TV and checked the weather, and every night the people on the weather said that tomorrow there would be terrible storms with loads and loads of thunder and lightning, but instead every day there was brilliant sunshine.

Finally, after six weeks of this, Dr Frankenstein got fed up, especially

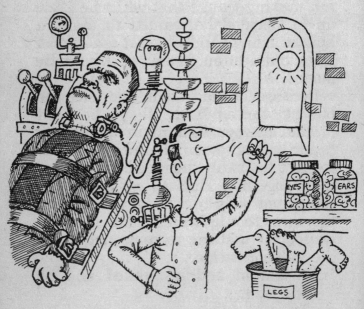

because the body of put-together parts was starting to go rotten, and already his neighbours had come round four times to complain about the smell.

So Dr Frankenstein wrote to the weather people to complain that they were all thick as bricks and wouldn't know what weather looked like if it came up and punched them in the eye. He threw his TV set in the dustbin, then went downstairs to his cellar to unplug his monster and throw it in the dustbin before the rats ate it. Just as he was about to unplug it . . . BOOOOOM! CRASHHHH! THUN-DERRRRR! POWWW! ZZZZZZZZZ!!! A terrible storm broke out, lightning went ZAPPPP!!! down the lightning rod, along the wires and, zapped through the monster!

The monster woke up, took one look at Dr Frankenstein, ate him, and then went off to create murder and mayhem throughout the rest of the world.

The moral of this story is: if the weather people tell you it's going to rain, it will, although it may take weeks for it to happen. If they tell you it's going to be good weather, don't believe them.

HOW TO DEAL WITH FRANKENSTEIN'S MONSTER

Because the monster looks so hideously ugly, people tend to try and deal with it by screaming loudly in fear, and then attacking it with cannons or axes or fire or equally dangerous objects.

In fact, all the monster wants is to be loved. If you should happen to meet it, smile, say, 'Hello, how are you today? My, but you're looking handsome. It's a real pleasure to meet you.'

The monster should be so pleased at this that it will smile back at you and give you a friendly pat on the shoulder, breaking your arm in at least two places. Do not take any notice of this, the monster does not mean to hurt you, it just doesn't know its own strength. Continue to be friendly, say, 'I know you didn't mean to hurt me, but I think you've accidentally broken my arm.'

The monster will be so overcome with grief and shame that it will cuddle you to try and make you feel better. When it does this it will then break all the rest of the bones in your body, so maybe it's better to just bash it hard and run off when you first meet it.

THE MONSTER THAT WAS MADE FROM A SUPERMARKET

Edward Frank N. Stein who lived in Birmingham was convinced that he was a descendant of the original Dr Frankenstein, and that he had inherited his ancestor's ability to make a monster come to life. As he had problems getting the bits to put together, he decided to make an animal monster out of bits from his local supermarket. So week by week, when he went shopping, he spent all his money buying more and more bits, until in the end he had:

one fish head

a neck of lamb

two shoulders of mutton

two crab's claws (for hands)

two legs of pork (with trotters for feet)

plus various bits for the insides: kidneys, liver, heart, etc.

Ed Stein then sewed all these bits together on his kitchen table. It took him days and days but finally he had a really horrible-looking monster all ready to plug in. He went out to his garage to get an extension lead to connect the monster up to the mains, and while he was out there rigging it all up, his family came home, casseroled his monster and ate it!

THE COMPUTER MONSTER

Little Frances Stein, aged two, was very advanced for her age, and her parents had given her a computer for

Christmas to help her progress even faster with her education. Part of the package was a program on human biology, making up a body from different parts.

Frances started the program going, and on the screen appeared all the bits: head, legs, arms, torso, and so on. Frances put them all together in almost the right order – although one arm was coming out of the top of the head – and the head was fixed to a foot.

Frances had just finished when there was a sudden CRASH SHAZAMM!! as a storm broke overhead and a flash of lightning hit the chimney of the Stein's house. There was a BANG! from Frances's computer – and the next second the creature JUMPED OFF THE COMPUTER SCREEN!!

'At last!!' cried the creature. 'I have been living scrambled up in that computer program for years! At last ... I am alive!! I am FREE!!!'

Unfortunately for the creature, as it rushed forward to leave the room and get out into the big wide world, it trod on its own head (which was on its foot) and killed itself.

The little boy monster came back to Dr Frankenstein's laboratory after a day at school in tears. When Frankenstein asked him what had upset him, the little boy monster said, 'The other kids at school say I've got a big head!'

'Don't take any notice of them,' said Frankenstein. 'Now, be a good little monster and go to the shops and get me some shopping so I can make soup for tea. I need ten kilos of tomatoes, ten kilos of onions and five litres of milk.'

'OK,' said the little boy monster. 'Shall I take a shopping bag?'

'No need,' said Frankenstein, 'just put them in your hat as usual.'

'Mummy, Mummy, why won't you play cards with me?'

'Because you keep throwing your hand in!'

5

ZOMBIES

WHAT IS A ZOMBIE?

A zombie is someone who is half-dead and half-alive. They get that way because their soul and their ability to think is taken from them, leaving them with just their body. Because they can't think any more, they just stand there until someone comes along and tells them what to do. This may cause you to think that all the rest of your class are zombies, and you will quite likely be right.

Zombies are also supposed to eat raw flesh. In fact zombies eat anything: people, animals, furniture, houses (although they have to eat them a brick at a time, and a few zombies have choked to death while trying to eat a front door without chewing it first).

WHERE ZOMBIES CAN BE FOUND

Before they are dug up (i.e. while they are still generally regarded as PZD (Pre-Zombie Dead), they live in coffins in graveyards and cause no trouble at all, because all they do is stay there and be dead.

However, once the Zombie Factor is activated and they clamber up out of the grave and start wandering around, then they can be absolutely anywhere. They never go back to their grave because they can no longer think, so they can't remember where their grave is. In fact they can't remember where *anything* is. Because of this they are very untidy: they drop things like hands and feet (because their bodies are dead they always have bits falling off them) and never pick them up. So ask yourself:

Are you untidy and forgetful? YES/NO.

Do you live in a grave? YES/NO.

If the answer to these questions is either YES or NO, then beware – YOU may be a ZOMBIE!!!

WHAT ZOMBIES ARE OFTEN DISGUISED AS TO FOOL PEOPLE:

– Train-spotters
– Teachers

– Traffic wardens

– People who watch nothing but day-time soap operas on TV

– Dentists

– People who keep insects as pets

– Kids whose noses are always dripping (which is actually their BRAIN trickling out of their nostrils!)

HOW TO DEAL WITH ZOMBIES

Because zombies are already dead, it is very difficult to stop them if they are coming towards you intent on eating you. They can't hear you if you say stop! They have no feeling in their bodies, so you can't hurt them. Even if you chainsaw one of a zombie's legs off (if you are that sort of person), it will not stop – it will simply carry on hopping towards you on its remaining leg. Even if you cut its remaining leg off, it will bounce towards you on its bum. Even if you cut a zombie's head off it will still keep coming at you.

The best way to deal with an approaching zombie is to pretend to be a zombie yourself, and then it will think you're not worth eating and will just stagger past you, arms out-stretched and with glazed eyes, looking for someone better to munch on. The trouble with this is that someone else passing by will think you really *are* a zombie, and then it'll be, 'Hand me that chainsaw, Wilbur, I think I got me a zombie here!' and next second it'll be GGZZZZZZZZZZZZ Ow! Ouch!!!

THE ZOMBIE WHO TRIED TO STOP SMELLING

Because zombies are dead they suffer from an embarrassing personal hygiene problem – as their flesh decays it begins to stink.

A decomposing zombie called Fred was very unhappy about the smell that was starting to come from him, so he went into a chemist shop and bought an underarm deodorant. Keen to get rid of his rotting smell as soon as possible, he went into an alley and lifted up his right arm to spray the deodorant on to his armpit – but unfortunately, his right arm fell off.

Holding the deodorant between his teeth, he then lifted up his left arm, and his left arm fell off.

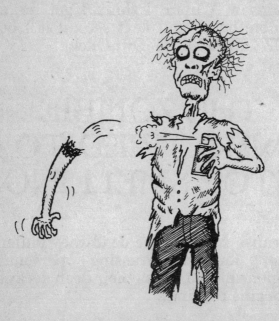

The unhappy Fred staggered back out into the street and bumped straight into a couple of kids.

'Aaaaaarghhh!!!' screamed one. 'It's a zombie!!'

'Don't worry,' said the other, 'he's armless.'

'Mummy, Mummy, what are the zombies having for dinner?'

'Shut up and get back in the oven.'

6

BLOBS

WHAT ARE BLOBS?

Blobs are those hideous squelchy shapeless things that you see in horror movies and videos. They either come from outer space or have been produced as the result of toxic wastes mixing together. They look like soggy rice pudding mixed with a transparent giant jellyfish.

They work by squelching in through a wall, or sliming their way under a door, and then taking over people and animals and so becoming a bigger and bigger blob, until they are so big they can Take Over The World.

WHERE BLOBS CAN BE FOUND (ORDINARY THINGS THAT CAN BE BLOBS IN DISGUISE)

Even though blobs end up so huge they can often smother a city, they usually start off as tiny blobs. They then have to feed off things (such as human beings, animals, etc) so that they can turn into a huge blob.

The sort of things that are often tiny blobs in disguise include:

– Nose-pickings

– Rice pudding

– Tapioca

– The yellow part of a fried egg

– Chewing gum

- Frog-spawn

- A pimple or other sort of spot

HOW TINY BLOBS TURN INTO BIG BLOBS

CHEWING GUM:

If a piece of chewing gum is really a tiny blob in disguise, it will stick to somewhere (the leg of a table, under a desk) just as if someone had put it there. Then it will gradually eat away at the thing (the table or desk), taking on its shape – until in the end the whole table or desk is actually A BLOB!

It will then wait for some human to come along and sit at it, and then it will gradually suck all the energy out of them and will take them over as well! To test this theory look around your class and at your teacher and ask yourself: Do any of them have blank expressions on their faces? Was there a blob of chewing gum stuck under their desk? If the answer is yes to both of these questions, then they have been turned into blobs!

FRIED EGGS:

Look at the fried egg on your plate. It looks ordinary, doesn't it? But some blobs have been known to arrive from outer space in the form of eggs. The

blob is the yellow bit. They sit on a plate and wait for the person eating the egg to bend over the plate, and then . . . ZPLAT!!! it jumps up off the plate and sticks to the face of the person and within seconds that person has turned into A BLOB!

NOSE-PICKINGS:

The worst blobs of all are those that are so tiny they can hide up your nose. The way they work is to suck your brain cells down through your nose bit

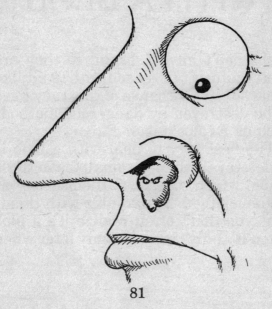

by bit until they have sucked up all your brain. There is only one way to get rid of them and that is to stick your finger up your nose and pick them out. Often when you do this adults will shout at you, 'Stop picking your nose!' This is because these adults are actually blobs themselves and they realize that you are trying to destroy one of their fellow creatures!

HOW TO DEAL WITH A BLOB

Blobs don't have a brain, so they are pretty difficult to reason with (a bit like some adults). Because of this they have to be destroyed by dangerous methods such as Explosions or Fire.

The best way to deal with a blob is to destroy it when it's small (as in those blobs which disguise themselves as nose-pickings). The trouble with this is that you don't often realize it's a blob when it's only tiny – it's only later when it's got so huge that it's about to eat your bedroom in one gulp that you realize it's actually a dangerous blob.

Also you will get into trouble if you start destroying small things (such as fried eggs, rice pudding, etc) because you think they may be blobs. The best thing to do is wait until they grow into huge blobs, and then let the adults take on the responsibility for dealing with them before they eat the planet. After all, it's their fault in the first place. If they had only listened to you . . . !

THE BLOB THAT STARTED OFF AS A STAIN ON A SHIRT

Little Terry Potts was a messy eater so his parents didn't think there was anything unusual about the spot of food on the front of his shirt. The next day Terry's mum noticed that he was still wearing the same dirty shirt, so she told him to take it off and put it in the laundry basket. If she had looked closer she would have noticed that the stain on the front of Terry's shirt had now grown BIGGER . . .

At the end of the week, Terry's mum opened the laundry basket to take out the washing, and as she took the lid off, she saw that all the laundry was now a bubbling slimy mass – it had turned into an ever-growing BLOB!

Thinking quickly, she grabbed a packet of a new washing powder that Promised To Get Rid Of All Unsightly Stains, and poured it straight into the laundry basket. There was a scream from inside the laundry basket, then the next second the blob shrivelled up and turned into a heap of smouldering charcoal.

THE BLOB THAT STARTED OFF AS PORRIDGE

Susan Sitz, aged eight, was about to eat a bowl of porridge at breakfast, when she thought she saw it move.

'Mum!' she said. 'There's something wrong with this porridge!'

'Shut up and eat it,' said her mum. 'You're always complaining.'

'I saw it move,' said Susan. 'I think it's trying to climb out of the bowl.'

'Nonsense!' said her mum. 'Now eat it up or I shall get very angry.'

So Susan ate it all up.

'There,' said her mum. 'All that fuss about nothing!'

And as her mum patted Susan on the head, her hand disappeared into a big slimy mass. Susan had turned into A BLOB!

THE BLOB THAT JUST WANTED TO BE FRIENDS

The newly-made blob opened one eye and looked out at the world from the crack in the pavement where it was hidden.

'Gosh!' it said. 'What a wonderful world this is! Isn't everything beautiful! Oh, if only I had a friend to share it with!'

It oozed its way out of the crack in

the pavement and saw a large lump of dog mess lying nearby on the pavement.

'Hullo!' it said. 'Will you be my friend?'

But the lump of dog mess said nothing.

The blob sighed and oozed its way across the pavement to the gutter. It was a rainy day and water was running along the gutter. The blob saw a glob of spit floating on top of the water.

'Hello!' said the blob. 'Will you be my friend?'

But the glob of spit just sailed past without speaking.

By now the blob was starting to get upset and more than a little bit angry.

'This world is a very unfriendly place,' growled the blob. 'But I will give it one last chance.'

It oozed along the pavement until it found the remains of a hamburger lying on the edge of the pavement, sticky with congealed tomato ketchup.

'Hello!' said the blob. 'Will you be my friend?'

Again there was no answer.

'That does it!' snapped the blob. 'You

try to be friendly and all they do is ignore you! Right – goodbye world!'

And, with that, the blob grew into the size of a large planet and swallowed the Earth in one gulp.

The moral of this story is: even blobs want to be loved!

'Mummy, Mummy, the other kids say I'm different and they can't bear to look at me.'

'Take no notice, son. Now just get back in your bottle and close the lid.'

7

ALIENS

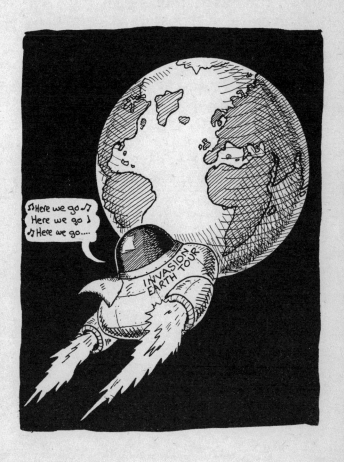

WHAT IS AN ALIEN?

An alien is a creature that has come from outer space and has landed on Earth. Why any self-respecting creature, with about ten zillion planets and a few million galaxies to choose from, would pick Earth to land on is one of the Great Mysteries of All Time. Various answers have been suggested as to why aliens land on Earth:

— They were heading for another planet but got lost

— They've run out of food on their home planet and Earth offers a good supply of food (particularly in human form)

— They've come as tourists

— They're collecting autographs of Famous Giraffes

— They bought Earth at an Inter-Galactic Auction

WHERE ALIENS CAN BE FOUND

Aliens can originally be found on their home planet. Once they get to Earth they have to hide – and where they hide depends on what they look like.

1. From the Planet Spud

These aliens look just like potatoes, and their spaceship is entirely made of decomposing organic matter. This serves a double purpose: it means it can't be detected by radar, and also when it lands it just looks like an ordinary compost heap. They land their spaceship in gardens and allotments. One imaginative team of Spudonauts got fed up with always landing on the same sort of place, so they landed their spaceship on a *motorway*. Unfortunately for them, it got flattened by a lorry, so as a result future teams of

Spudonauts went back to landing in gardens and allotments.

2. From the Planet Brick

The Planet Brick is made entirely of brick dust, and the creatures who live on it are composed of bricks. Why on Earth these creatures should want to travel to Earth is baffling, but we suppose they get fed up with looking at nothing but brick dust day after day. Their spaceships look like big buildings, and they just land them in a city or a big town, go out for a walk and take a few photos, and then go back home again. This is one of the reasons why people on Earth notice, one day, that a building that was there the day before, has now gone: the truth is that it was just a Planet Brick spaceship parking there.

It is rumoured that these Brick People come to Earth on Eating Holidays, and munch their way through bungalows and old castles as a change from their monotonous diet of brick dust. This is possibly the reason why so many old buildings look like they are falling down – the Brick People have chewed them away.

3. From the Planet Vomit

These are really dangerous creatures because their aim is to Take Over The World, and they are planning to do it by the following cunning method:

a. Cover the pavements of the world's major cities with puddles of vomit.

b. When two puddles of vomit get next to each other a chemical reaction is set off that makes them join together and come alive.

c. The secret agents already on Earth who are working for Planet Vomit then scoop up that living lump of vomit and hide it in a cupboard and let it grow.

d. When it has grown big enough they dress it up in human clothes.

e. They get it elected to government where it can order humans around. In this way they intend to Dominate The World. The way to stop them is: Don't Vote For Them!

4. From the Planet Can

The creatures who live on the Planet Can are made of metal and look just like soft-drink cans. The protective clothing they wear is a thin layer of paint of different colours, with the name of the maker written on it. Their spaceships are round and made of metal. Because of this they are very noticeable, so spaceships from Planet Can like to land on beaches where they can burrow beneath the sand.

You can always tell if you are on a beach that has a Planet Can spaceship hidden beneath it because it will be covered with the dead bodies of crew members who went out exploring and collapsed from starvation before they could make it back to their ship.

HOW TO DEAL WITH ALIENS

This depends on two things:

A. What The Aliens Want

B. How Big They Are.

If they have just turned up on Earth because they are lost and want directions, then show them the way to get

to Alpha Centauri, or Jupiter, or wher-
ever it is they are heading for, and
wave them goodbye.

If, on the other hand, they are here
to Take Over The Earth, then what you
do next depends on B. How Big They
Are!

If they are ant-sized then treading
on their spaceship should solve the
problem.

If they are Enormous Monsters As
Big As A House With Bug-Eyes And
Lots Of Tentacles, then treading on
their spaceship will not have much
impact in stopping them. To defeat
them you will need to use Cunning
Methods:

1. Pretend that human beings are actually a sub-species and that the Earth
is really dominated by television sets.
The aliens will then aim their blasters
(or whatever weapons they are using)
at the TV sets and demand that they
surrender. The TVs will ignore them
and will just go on nattering away and
showing pictures of toys and soft-drink
bottles and soap operas. The aliens will
then have to decide whether to wipe

out every TV on Earth, or accept defeat and move on to another planet and try to conquer that.

2. Tell the aliens that the Earth is actually just a moon of the hot planet which it goes round, which is called the Sun, and that if the aliens want to rule the Earth they have to go to the Sun and conquer the Sun People first. The aliens will set off for the Sun, and by the time they find out you've tricked them they will have melted.

3. Get everyone on Earth to treat the aliens as if they are children dressed

up as aliens, by saying things like, 'Come on, John! Take off that costume and wash your hands, it's time for tea!', etc. Eventually the aliens will start to believe it must be true, and will start doing things like washing their hands, going to bed early, wanting to watch horror videos, etc.

An alien from outer space teleported to Earth, materialized next to a petrol pump and asked it for directions. When it got no answer, it snapped, 'Take your finger out of your ear – I'm talking to you!'

'Mummy, Mummy, the other kids at school say I'm different.'

'Shut up and don't worry your little heads about it.'

8

THE YETI!
(and other hideous creatures of the unknown)

WHAT IS A YETI?

The yeti is also known as The Abominable Snowman. It is a huge hairy monster and it looks a lot like your dad would if he never shaved and never had his hair cut. It lives high up in snowy mountains and keeps out of sight of people. Some people say this is because it is incredibly shy. Others say it is because the yeti is a miserable grump who doesn't like mixing.

WHAT IS A BIGFOOT?

Bigfoot is said to be a huge hairy monster that lives in the mountain forests of Canada, and is supposed to be related to the yeti. Quite what sort of relation to the yeti bigfoot is, no one quite seems to know. It is unlikely they are very close family as they don't see a lot of each other. In fact it is said that they have hardly anything to do with each other at all.

There are various rumours why this should be: one rumour says that the bigfoot family used to write postcards to the yeti family at Cave Number Three, Everest, Himalayas, Tibet, but got fed up with never getting a reply. The reason no reply was ever received was because: 1. the yeti family couldn't read and write; and 2. the yeti family used to eat the postmen, thus causing the remaining Everest postmen to go on strike.

WHAT IS A TROLL?

A troll is a creature that is made of stone and covered with hair. Like the yeti and the bigfoot it keeps out of the way of people, preferring to live in deep forests.

Trolls are also said to hide under bridges and sing songs at goats who try to get across. This is actually not true. The rumour was started because one particular troll, on realizing that he was made out of stone, decided he had the right qualifications to be a *rock* singer, and so he started singing. The rest of his tribe of trolls all suffered earache because his singing was so bad, so they stuck him under a bridge five kilometres outside the troll village. It was this bridge that the local goats used to go over on their way to their ballet-dancing classes. The troll's singing was so bad that all the goats stopped going to ballet lessons, and as

BEWARE! TROLL SINGING

a result there were soon no goats in the Norwegian National Ballet Company, a loss that is still felt to this day.

WHERE YETI, BIGFOOT AND TROLLS CAN BE FOUND

1. Yeti
The yeti (or abominable snowman) lives at the top of snowy mountains, places like Mount Everest in the Himalayas. Sightings have also been made at the South Pole, the North Pole and inside the fridge at the Acme Ice Cream Corporation, where the yeti went for his holidays.

2. Bigfoot
Bigfoot lives in the mountain forests of Canada. Sightings have also been made in shoe shops in Toronto and Quebec, particularly in the Extra Large Department.

3. Troll

Trolls live mainly in Scandinavia, although they have been seen in places with Scandinavian connections: sitting in a field of swedes and in the audience at a performance of *Hamlet, Prince of Denmark*.

HOW TO DEAL WITH THE YETI, BIGFOOT AND TROLLS

Say to it in either Himalayan (if it's a yeti), Canadian (if it's a bigfoot) or Scandinavian (if it's a troll): 'Hi! My name is *(whatever your name is)* and you could be a big star. Let me be your agent. Just sign this contract that gives me 99% of all the money you earn.'

When the creature has signed the contract, take it with you on a bus round all the TV stations. They will be so excited they will pay you large sums of money just for a few minutes of air time with your creature. A typical TV interview will go like this:

INTERVIEWER: This morning we are lucky to have with us in the studio a troll from the remote forests of Scandinavia. Tell me, what's it like being a troll?

TROLL: Nnnggg.

INTERVIEWER: Really! That's fascinating! Now, what does a troll like you look for in a girlfriend?

TROLL: Nnnggg.

INTERVIEWER: Wonderful! And do you have a favourite troll recipe that you'd like to share with the viewers?

TROLL: Nnnggg.

INTERVIEWER: What about clothes? I can see that you're wearing a very unusual outfit, made – as far as I can tell – only of hair. Do you have any fashion tips that you'd like to pass on to our lucky viewers?

TROLL: Nnnggg.

INTERVIEWER: That's brilliant! And finally, who do you think will win the World Cup?

TROLL: Norway.

THE 'NOT VERY ABOMINABLE' SNOWMAN

This was a yeti who was a member of the famous Abominable Snowman Family, only he was rejected by the tribe because he wasn't abominable at all. In fact he was known scornfully by them as The Quite Nice Snowman Really. When he discovered weak and feeble travellers lying frozen high up in the Himalayas, instead of eating them and trundling off, leaving behind a pile of bones and one large footprint in the snow like all other abominable snowmen, The Quite Nice Snowman Really would say, 'Hello, you must be lost,' and would help the traveller back down the mountain, and had even been known to telephone for the ambulance.

THE BIGFOOT WHO WAS CAST OUT OF HIS TRIBE

When Ben Bigfoot was born he was a normal healthy hairy ugly monster and his parents were delighted. As he grew bigger they noticed a shocking thing about him – his feet didn't grow very big. In fact, his feet remained SMALL! The biggest they ever got – and this was when he was seventeen – were size six!

The Bigfeet held an emergency meeting and told the unhappy Ben he would have to leave – they couldn't allow a Bigfoot with small feet to be around, it would ruin their reputation. So Ben

was forced to go away and roam the wastes of the Canadian forests on his small feet.

As he wandered he came upon a group of lumberjacks chopping down trees.

'Aaaaarghhh!!!' they yelled, 'It's Bigfoot!' (which only proves they didn't take a very close look at Ben's feet).

The lumberjacks ran off in fear, and Ben began to go after them to point out to them how wrong they were, that actually he was a *smallfoot*, when a tree that one of the lumberjacks had been in the middle of cutting down fell down and landed on Ben's feet.

'OW!!!' yelled Ben.

He pushed the tree off his feet – and as he looked at his feet his heart was filled with happiness – because the tree had squashed them as flat as pancakes – and they were now at least a size twenty-five!

Straight away Ben hurried back to his own tribe – flip-flapping on his big feet as he went – and was welcomed by them with open arms as a true Bigfoot.

THE OVER-SENSITIVE TROLL

Og the over-sensitive troll lived in a forest in Norway, but he was very unhappy because he felt that all the trees were whispering about him behind his back, saying things like, 'Isn't Og ugly?' and 'Why do we have to live next door to a troll?' He became so sensitive about all this whispering that he decided to move somewhere where there were no trees to talk about him, so (because trolls are made of stone) he jumped on board a shipment of rocks bound for the deserts of Saudi Arabia.

At first he felt quite happy in the desert, but then he started to hear whispering sounds at night, and he started to think that the sand dunes were talking about him, saying things like, 'This used to be a nice neighbourhood until that troll moved in.'

So, Og headed back to Norway on the next boatload of rocks, and as it sailed into a fjord, he rolled over the side and plunged into the water, determined to end it all.

However, trolls can't die because they're made of stone, and so poor Og sank to the bottom of the fjord, and there he sits to this day, listening to the fishes swimming past him and whispering horrible things about him behind his back.

'Mummy, Mummy, there's a cannibal outside asking for help.'

'OK, you can give him a hand.'

9

MONSTERS FROM THE DEEP

WHAT IS A MONSTER FROM THE DEEP?

Monsters from The Deep vary in size. There are weird sea creatures, such as the Terrifying Inflatable Cod, which is the result of accidentally cross-breeding a cod with an inflatable Lilo. The Terrifying Inflatable Cod can block up its gills and blow itself up from a small ordinary cod into something the size of a blue whale. At the other end of the scale are those creatures which are HUGE to begin with and live right at the bottom of the deepest ocean. They are very rarely seen as they are quite happy living far down in The Deep, usually sleeping, and are only brought to the surface as the result of something like a nuclear explosion at the bottom of the sea (caused by some idiotic government testing nuclear

weapons). When this happens the monster gets pretty fed up at being disturbed and comes up to the surface to 'kick ass' and make life really rather unpleasant for those who woke it up.

WHERE MONSTERS FROM THE DEEP CAN BE FOUND

In the sea, obviously, you idiot!

HOW TO DEAL WITH A MONSTER FROM THE DEEP

This depends on how big the monster is.

If it's just fish-size then the best thing is to send out a fishing boat to catch it in a net.

However, if it's a Huge Angry

Monster, then trying to catch it in a net is only going to annoy it even more, and it will quite likely eat the boat – crew and all. In cases like this the only answer is to treat it in the same way as a giant blob, which is to ZAP it with every weapon the planet can rustle up.

THE INVASION OF THE TWO-HEADED KILLER SHARKS

As a result of a nuclear submarine breaking up in a tropical ocean, a shoal of killer sharks mutated overnight and all developed two heads! This meant that they now had twice the number of killer jaws, and were twice as dangerous as before.

Being two-headed also gave them twice the brain power, and their new powerful brains led them to think that if they wanted to keep eating well the answer was to go to where people were: a packed holiday beach. So off they swam, mouths agape and stomachs at the ready.

Luckily for the unsuspecting holiday-makers, the fact that the sharks had two heads led to the invasion coming to nothing – because as the sharks got closer to land, the heads began to argue with each other: the left head of one shark saying, 'I think we ought to go to Brighton,' and its right head saying, 'Spain is better at this time of year.'

The other sharks also started arguing in the same way, and in the end the heads began to eat each other and the invasion vanished, eaten by itself.

THE BEAST FROM .000025 OF A FATHOM

Once upon a time, at the bottom of the village pond in a village called Little Twitt, there lived a frog. One day this frog was sitting on the bottom of the pond minding its own business, when a comic that some passing litter lout had thrown away fell into the pond and sank, landing next to the frog. The frog looked at the cover. The title of the comic read: 'THE BEAST FROM 500 FATHOMS!' and showed a picture of an enormous amphibian creature, kicking the daylights out of a block of flats, and generally giving human beings a hard time.

The frog sat there, looking at the comic and remembering all the troubles he had had from humans, and at that moment the frog was filled with an inspiration to follow in the beast's footsteps.

'I shall rise from the deep and have revenge on behalf of persecuted pond-dwellers!' bubbled the frog.

With that he swam to the surface, leapt out of the pond and stood firmly on the road that passed the pond, back legs fixed defiantly to the road, his front legs folded across his chest.

'Come humans and tremble in fear!' he croaked, 'because I am the beast of .000025 of a fathom, and I have come to bash up your buildings and knock you all about! You may attack me with your worst weapons, but they will not harm me, because I am invincible!'

And as he stood there defiantly there came a rumbling sound, and then the Post Office van came rolling around the bend in the road and squashed him flat.

THE KILLER OCTOPUSS

The killer octopuss is a fierce cat called Tibbles that has eight teeth.

Because it only has eight teeth (all of which are at the back) it isn't an enormously successful hunter, but it has a very savage suck and can empty a carton of milk in five seconds. It may not have actually killed a living being, but it has destroyed four armchairs and a settee.

Strictly speaking it shouldn't be in this section at all because it doesn't live underwater. However, it does live deep down in the cellar of Number 22 Acacia Gardens, Luton, whose owners have offered us a Large Bribe if we mention Tibbles in this book. So:

'Hello, Tibbles, The Killer Octopuss From The Deep!!'

'Mummy, Mummy, there's a fish in the piano.'

'OK, I'll call the tuna out.'

10

GHOSTS

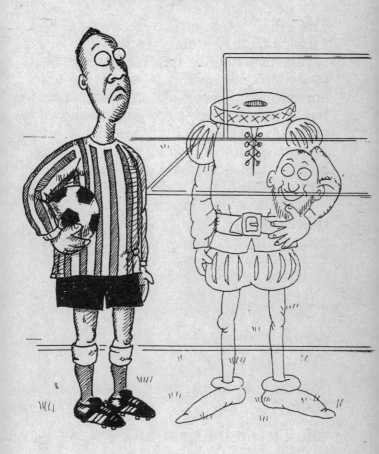

WHAT IS A GHOST?

A ghost is a spooky thing that can walk through solid walls. Some people think that a ghost is the spirit of someone or something that is dead, but that is only half the story; you can also get ghosts of people and things that are still alive!

Have you ever been walking along a street and thought you'd seen a friend of yours, but you know that they're supposed to be somewhere else – like at home or at school. What you have seen is the ghost of your friend – even though they're still alive!

Further proof of this is as follows: You know that your cat – which is black with white bits – is at home fast asleep, but when you are out you see a cat that is exactly the same! Or you go into a friend's house and you see a table in their living room that is *exactly* the same as the one in your house! In both these cases what you have seen is a ghost!

This is because when people or animals go to sleep, their spirit can get up and go for a stroll. In the case of things like tables and chairs and knives and forks, they are always asleep so their spirits are always wandering about.

Where dead people come into the picture is this: someone falls asleep and their spirit steps out of their body and goes for a walk, and while the spirit is out, the body drops dead for some reason. When the spirit comes back it finds no body, and so has to carry on walking about.

This is why people report that they have seen the ghost of a famous person from history – such as King Henry VIII, or Cleopatra, or Ug the Neanderthal. What happened in most of those cases was that the Famous Historical Person got bumped off while they were fast asleep, by some extremely nasty rival.

WHERE GHOSTS CAN BE FOUND

All over the place, really, though most ghosts hang around the place where they last saw their body in case they remember where they put it.

Because of this you tend to find the ghosts of kings and queens in royal palaces, the ghosts of tables and chairs in furniture shops, and the ghost of a tin of tuna fish at the bottom of the sea.

HOW TO DEAL WITH GHOSTS

Some people think they have to get tough with ghosts and bring in a person called an exorcist to get rid of them. This exorcist does all sorts of horrible things to the ghost, like chanting in a loud voice and shouting and throwing lighted candles and Bibles at it.

All this is a bit unnecessary. Ghosts can't actually hurt you because they are just spirits – thin air in the shape of a person or a thing. For this reason there is no need to be afraid of them.

Ghosts are also often very sad because they may have been hanging around in the same place for thousands of years with no one to talk to. Frankly they are bored and all they want is a bit of sympathy. So, if you meet a ghost, be kind to it. Talk to it. Ask how it is. Give it your opinion of what the weather has been up to lately. Tell it what is happening on your favourite

TV soap opera. Sing it your favourite song. Show it your collection of felt-tip pens. All that should get rid of it pretty swiftly.

THE GHOST WHO WANTED TO RULE THE WORLD

Once upon a time there lived a tyrant who wanted to Rule the World. He was an evil and powerful man who used to bump off his enemies (which was nearly everyone else), until in the end he ruled nearly all the world and everyone was afraid of him. Being a tyrant, he was always afraid that one of his assistants would try and take his power from him. So, having bumped off most of his enemies, he started bumping off his friends by pretending that they were traitors. His friends became a bit upset at this as, one by one, they started to disappear. So one night, five of them got together and bumped the tyrant off as he slept.

The next morning the tyrant woke up, ready to start a heavy day's world domination, but found that when he started to give people orders, no one took any notice of him. The tyrant was *furious* and started shouting louder and louder and threatening to have people bumped off all over the place. But still no one took any notice of him, and it was only when he saw the posters announcing his funeral that he realized what had happened – he was dead!

The tyrant was most upset when he discovered this. He went off to his ex-friends and began to shout at them – but they ignored him, just like everybody else did.

As time went by the ex-tyrant carried on shouting at people, giving them orders, but as no one seemed to take any notice of him he started to change. He still shouted at people, giving them orders, but instead of giving them orders like, 'Destroy this or that

country!' or 'Take over the world!' he
started shouting things like 'Clean up
the bathroom after you've used it!' and
'Don't leave your comics lying around
on the floor!'

Now he is reduced to a ghostly voice
which can be heard at bus-stops shouting at bus drivers, 'Why is this bus so
late!' It's a long way from Ruling The
World, but that's what happens to
tyrants after they die.

THE GHOST WHO WAS A FAILURE

The worst failure in the history of ghosts was the ghost of a young man called Simple Sid. Simple Sid was a friendly and happy village idiot when he was alive, and after he died, he carried on, being a Ghost Idiot. He was such an idiot that when he went for a walk in a haunted house he opened doors instead of walking through them.

The other ghosts got annoyed with Sid being such an idiot because he was ruining the reputation of *all* ghosts. Instead of being frightened when people saw Sid, they laughed at him, particularly because he kept on being so happy and friendly with everyone.

The other ghosts decided to teach Sid how to be scary. For a start they taught him how to take off his head. The trouble was that when Sid did this he forgot where he put it, so he then walked around headless and kept bumping through things.

The other ghosts held a meeting over what to do about Sid; half of them voted to get rid of him by bumping him off, but the other half reminded them that he was a ghost already, so that was impossible, so they had to admit they were forced to live with him.

So, if you ever go into a haunted house and find a ghost who greets you with a happy smile, climbs over walls instead of walking through them, asks you if you've seen his head lately and then makes you laugh by telling you Ghost Jokes, like: 'What do ghosts like for dinner? . . . Spook-etti!', then you've just met Sid!

THE GHOST IN YOUR TV SET

Have you ever noticed sometimes when you're watching TV that there occasionally seems to be a fuzzy shadowy outline around some of the actors. If you ask your parents, they'll say, 'Oh, that's just a ghost in the picture.' Well, here is how that ghost got into your TV set.

When television was first invented there was an actress called Sarah Figgis who was determined to get on it and be famous. Unfortunately she was such a terrible actress that no one would allow her anywhere near the TV studios. In her attempts to get past security and into the studio she disguised herself as a camerawoman, a cleaner and even as a horse. But each time (because she was such a terrible actress) she was spotted and thrown out.

Finally, she could stand it no more and one day when a programme was being made about electricity, she rushed into the studio, threw herself in front of the cameras and was electro-cuted on the spot! Her ghost, on the other hand, got caught up in the air-waves, and her spirit was trapped ever after, in every TV channel.

So, whenever you see a shadowy picture on your TV set, you can say, 'That's Sarah Figgis. She finally made it!'

'Mummy, Mummy, the other kids say I'm a ghost.'

'Shut up, and stop walking through that wall.'

11

WITCHES

WHAT IS A WITCH?

OLD-FASHIONED WITCHES

Old-fashioned witches were easily recognized:

– They wore long black cloaks

– On their heads they wore tall pointed black hats (to fit their tall pointed heads)

– They rode in the sky on broomsticks

– They had a cat with them as their assistant

– They had hideously ugly faces

– Their fingernails were so long their hands looked like claws

– They mixed their spells in a large cauldron over a log fire

MODERN WITCHES

Modern witches are not so easily recognized:

– They wear jogging gear

– On their heads they wear crash-helmets

– They ride in the sky in a mini-heli-copter

– They have an android with them as their assistant – this android is often cunningly disguised as a human being

– They take care of their looks because they use all the cosmetics as advertised on TV

– They have their nails manicured

– They mix their spells in a food mixer

The thing is, this is really unfair of the modern witch. In the old days when you saw a witch coming you screamed and ran away. Nowadays you see a witch and you don't recognize her, and on April Fool's Day you say to yourself: 'There's some ordinary woman wearing a crash-helmet and walking around with her husband who looks like an android – let's play a trick on her,' and you call out, 'You've got your shoes on upside down!'

The next second, before you can call out, 'April Fool!' there's a SHAZAM! and a POW! as lightning leaps out from her fingertips, and then you're hopping around on the pavement going, 'Rivet, rivet, rivet', and doing all the other things that frogs do.

In fact, most witches have no sense of humour. If you tell them a joke about witches, even a harmless one like, 'What's the difference between a witch and the letters M A K E S? ... one makes spells and the other spells *makes*.' Instead of smiling politely (because the joke is so terrible) like most adults do, a witch will go SHAZAM! and a POW!, etc and turn ou into a brick!

WHERE WITCHES CAN BE FOUND

OLD-FASHIONED WITCHES

Old-fashioned witches were nearly always found in a tiny cottage deep in some wood, where they wait for some unsuspecting little children to come and knock on the door so they could put them in a pie. Or they would be in a cave, surrounded by bats, while they made some horrible thick soup in a cauldron. This soup was usually made out of things like wing of bat, head of snake, eye of frog, toe of newt, blood of monster, etc – a bit like school dinners really!

MODERN WITCHES

Modern witches are nearly always found on TV chat shows talking about their talents and how strong their powers are. If their powers are so strong then why aren't these chat shows at the top of the TV charts? That's what we want to know!

HOW TO DEAL WITH A WITCH

Be nice to them and hope they'll be nice back to you in return.

This is the only way to deal with a witch, because you don't know what powers they may have. For all you know they could be so powerful that, if you start trying to get rid of them, they could turn you into something really awful – like a train-spotter!

If a witch is causing you problems (turning your family into toads, etc) You can always try to hire a witch of your own as a method of defence. Then let the pair of them blast at each other with spells and incantations – and hope your witch wins.

THE WITCH WHO COULDN'T LEARN TO FLY HER BROOM

A witch called Annie had terrible trouble trying to learn to fly her broom – even though she took over a hundred flying lessons she kept failing her Broom Test. Her problem was that she kept saying the spell for 'Reverse' when she meant to say the spell for 'Turn Left', and her braking wasn't too good either.

Finally, a friend said to her, 'Tell you what – why don't you try learning to drive on an automatic.' So Annie went out and bought a vacuum cleaner and her flying improved enormously!

Annie now only has one problem with her flying – she can't go very far on the vacuum cleaner because the lead isn't long enough.

THE WITCH WHO MADE HER SPELLS IN A MICROWAVE OVEN

There once was a witch who was fed up with the very long time it took to mix her magic potions in her cauldron. By the time she got the mixtures to boiling point it was often time for her to go to bed.

Then she saw an advert which said: 'Buy a Microwave Oven and cut your cooking time by 95%!!' So she bought herself a microwave, and then she decided she could save even more time if she cooked up more than one spell in her microwave at the same time!

Unfortunately for her, she didn't read the instructions properly, she just threw five different magic potions into the microwave and switched it on.

Then she went away and left it, to go and check on her magic herbs. While she was out of the house the microwave blew up, blowing the mixed-up magic potions all over the house.

When she returned to her house the witch was shocked to find the following:

– Her Magic Potion For Making Things Bigger now made things smaller, and all her furniture could now fit into a matchbox

– Her Love Potion had splashed on her pet crow and had caused it to fall in love with her kettle

– Her Beauty Magic now gave warts and pimples to everyone who used it

– Her cat had turned into a giraffe

The witch was so angry, she sent her microwave back to its makers and demanded her money back. When they wouldn't give it to her, she turned everyone who worked for the company into sheep, and the company went out of business.

'Mummy, Mummy, the other kids say you're a witch?'

'Shut up, I'm trying to reverse this broom.'

How do you make a witch scratch?

Take away her 'w'!

What do you call people who try to thumb a lift at Halloween?

Witchhikers!

How does a witch tell the time?

With a witch watch!

What do you call a witch who lives by the sea?

A sandwitch!

12

THE END BIT

OK, now you know all that there is to be known about Monsters And How To Deal With Them. So, this is the, Final Check-List Of Things You Will Need To Take With You Before You Get Out There And Get Monster Hunting!

VAMPIRES

– Wooden stake for bashing through heart

– Hammer for hitting wooden stake

– Garlic

– Cross

– Jug of water

– Torch for Instant Sunlight

– Bottle of blood to keep vampire busy if it goes wrong

– Plaster for neck in case you get bitten

WEREWOLVES

- Silver bullet

- Gun to fire silver bullet from

- Dog biscuits

- Dog lead

- Bone

- A fat appetizing friend in case it goes wrong

THE MUMMY

- A T-shirt that says, 'Cleopatra Was My Friend'

- Instant starch that will make the mummy's bandages go so stiff it can't move

- A dustpan and brush (for sweeping the mummy up if it falls apart)

FRANKENSTEIN'S MONSTER

– A spanner and screwdriver (for undoing the bolt that holds its head on)

– A friendly smile

– A large sledgehammer (in case the Friendly Smile doesn't work)

ZOMBIES

– A peg (to put in your nose because of the smell)

– A garden fork (for picking up the zombie when it falls apart)

– A grave (to put the zombie in)

BLOBS

– A thing for scraping it off your shoe when you tread in it

– A bucket for putting the blob in

ALIENS

– An Intergalactic Phrase Book so you can talk to them in their own language (it is no use shouting, 'Hands up!' at them if they think you're really saying, 'I want you to punch me in the ear!')

– A Supersonic Alien Blaster

YETIS, BIGFEET, TROLLS

– A camera (because otherwise no one will ever believe you really found a yeti or a bigfoot or a troll)

– A suit of body armour as protection against being crushed when hugged in greeting by the yeti

MONSTERS FROM THE DEEP

– A fishing rod

– A net

– Bait (eg a worm)

GHOSTS

– Food for bait (ghosts' favourite food includes Spooketti and Dreaded Wheat)

– A vacuum cleaner (for sucking the ghost into)

– A jar or bottle (for keeping the ghost in after you've caught it)

WITCHES

– A book of spells

– A dog (to protect you from the witch's cat)

– A Broomstick De-Stabilizer and Puncture Outfit (for puncturing broomsticks, not for mending them)

There, now you're all set, so Good Luck with your Monster Hunting. But, before you go, one final word of warning . . .

As soon as you are seen walking around carrying all the above equipment, some people are going to get suspicious. Word will get around about What You Are Up To. And, when that happens, all the monsters in your area will get worried. They might well decide that there is only one way to protect themselves, and that is to go out and hunt . . .

YOU

AAAARGHHHH!!!!!

Join the RED FOX Reader's Club

The Red Fox Reader's Club is for readers of all ages. All you have to do is ask your local bookseller or librarian for a Red Fox Reader's Club card. As an official Red Fox Reader you only have to borrow or buy eight Red Fox books in order to qualify for your own Red Fox Reader's Clubpack – full of exciting surprises! If you have any difficulty obtaining a Red Fox Reader's Club card please write to: Random House Children's Books Marketing Department, 20 Vauxhall Bridge Road, London SW1V 2SA.

Other great reads *from* **Red Fox**

Giggle and groan with a Red Fox humour book!

Nutty, naughty and quite quite mad, the Red Fox humour list has a range of the silliest titles you're likely to see on a bookshelf! Check out some of our weird and wonderful books and we promise you'll have a ribticklingly good read!

MIAOW! THE CAT JOKE BOOK – Susan Abbott

Be a cool cat and paws here for the purrfect joke! Get your claws into this collection of howlers all about our furry friends that will have you feline like a grinning Cheshire Cat!

ISBN 0 09 998460 1 £1.99

THE SMELLY SOCKS JOKE BOOK – Susan Abbott

Hold your nose . . . here comes the funniest and foulest joke book you're likely to read for a while! Packed with pungent puns and reeking with revolting riddles, this one is guaranteed to leave you gasping for air!

ISBN 0 09 956270 7 £1.99

TUTANKHAMUN IS A BIT OF A MUMMY'S BOY
– Michael Coleman

Have you ever dreaded taking home your school report or a letter from the Head? You're in good company! Did you know that Shakespeare was really "hopeless at English" and that Christopher Columbus had "absolutely no sense of direction"? There's fifty other previously unpublished school reports which reveal hilarious secrets about the famous which not many people know . . .

ISBN 0 09 988180 2 £2.99

THE FISH AND CHIPS JOKE BOOK – Ian Rylett

This book comes complete with a fish-and-chips scratch and sniff panel so you can sniff while you snigger at this delicious collection of piping-hot pottiness! Your tastebuds will be tickled no end with this mouth-watering concoction of tasty gags so tuck into a copy today! It's a feast of fun!

ISBN 0 09 995040 5 £2.99